A WOLF'S TALE

Eva
Montanari

This edition published by Parragon Books Ltd in 2014 and distributed by

Parragon Inc.
440 Park Avenue South, 13th Floor
New York, NY 10016
www.parragon.com

Text and Illustrations © Eva Montanari

PaRragon

Bath · New York · Cologne · Melbourne · Delhi
Hong Kong · Shenzhen · Singapore · Amsterdam

ISBN 978-1-4723-0721-7

Printed in China

Gather round, little ones, don't be afraid.
I'm going to tell you a story.

My great-great-great-great-grandfather
was a very bad wolf. Do you remember
the story of the three little pigs?
You know, the ones with the houses made
of straw, sticks, and bricks? And do you
remember the wolf who huffed and puffed
and blew their houses down?
Well, that was him.

But this story is about me ...

I've lived here, above Pig City, for many years.
Watching. Waiting.

Then, one summer's day, as a breeze
was blowing over Pig City,
I noticed the little pigs
were up to something.
They were whispering
and reading notes.
Suddenly …

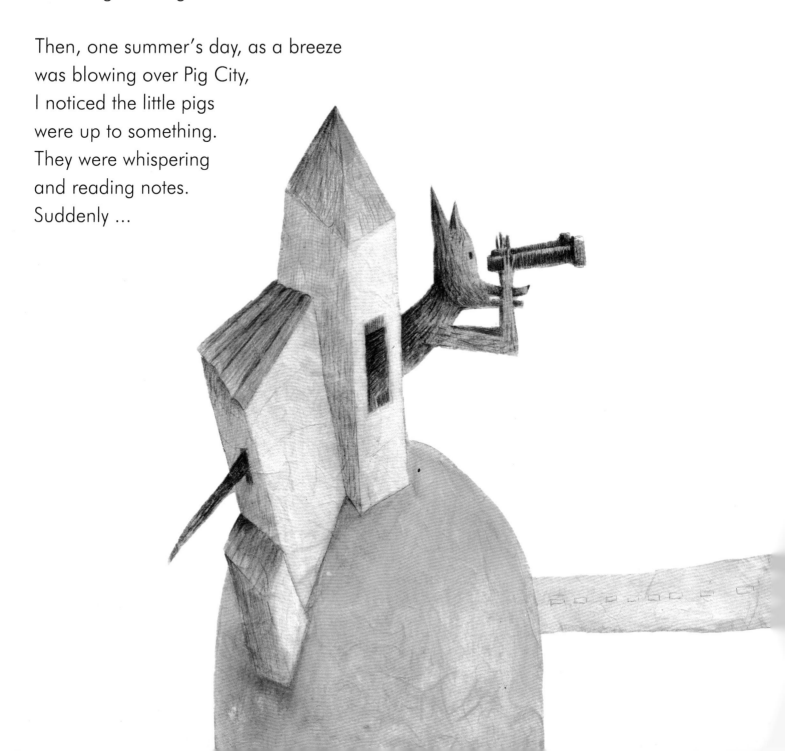

A whispery wind caught a note

~ Invitation ~
You are invited to
Little Pig's
surprise birthday party.
Today, 4 o'clock,
Brick House.

and blew it right up to my window!

Finally, I had my chance!
I got straight to work,
preparing a little surprise
of my own ...

I worked hard all day, until I saw the little pigs
scurrying across town, making their way
to the party.

So, with my surprise ready, I crept
down the hill after them ...

Pig City
was huge!

I wandered the streets …

...but I couldn't find Brick House anywhere.

So I knocked on a door.

"Please, Mrs. Pig, can you tell me where Brick House is?" I asked. "I've got a surprise for them."

"No, no, no! Not by the hair of my chinny-chin-chin!" screeched the pig inside.

Knock, Knock, Knock!

I walked further, my package feeling heavier, but I still couldn't find Brick House.

So I knocked on
another door.

"Please, Mr. Pig, can you tell me
where Brick House is?" I asked.
"I've got a surprise for them."
"No, no, no! Not by the hair of my
chinny-chin-chin!" boomed
the pig inside.

Knock,
Knock,
Knock!

I walked even further and, just as I was
about to give up, I saw it—Brick House!

"Please, little pigs, little pigs, can I come in?" I asked. *"I've got a surprise for you."*

"No, no, no, not by the hairs of our chinny-chin-chins!" squealed the little pigs inside.

"Please little pigs," I asked again. "I've brought something for you ..."

Knock,
Knock,
Knock!

I heard running and squeaking,
but no one let me in.

The walk had been long and my package was heavy.
Tired and fed up, I pushed and pushed against
the door ...

And slowly it creaked open!

"Don't be afraid little pigs. You see, I've brought you something. It's big ... and it's bright ... and I made it just for you. It's a ..."

That day, the little pigs let me join their party ...

and the only huffing
and puffing was for
the candles!

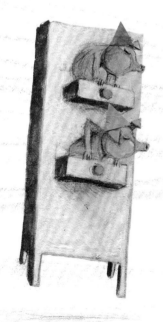

So you see, little ones,
my great-great-great-great-grandfather
was a very bad wolf. But I'm not!
And now, little pigs and big,
not-so-bad wolves can live
happily ever after ...

... together!

It's bedtime, the story
is over. And I hope you're
all sleepy, otherwise
I'll HUFF ... and
I'll PUFF ...
and I'll ...

EAT
YOU
ALL
UP!
Just kidding.